BIG BLACK AND WORSHIPED

Straight to Gay BBC First Time

Michael Levi

ISBN: 9798440249035
Imprint: Independently published

2nd edition

Cover design by: Michael Levi

CONTENTS

CHAPTER 1

"Once you go black, you never go back" was one of the jokes my ex-girlfriend always told me. Her intent was to make me laugh, but whenever I did so, I wasn't being genuine about it.

Her name was Jessica and she was a total babe. Relatively tall for a woman, perfect black hair, smooth and tanned skin, nice curves, intelligent, and had a cute face. She had it all and maybe because of that, she decided I wasn't good enough for her.

Meanwhile, I was on the short side when it came to height. Alongside that, I was of average build, had brown hair and eyes, and a baby face most girls adored.

I had no idea why she gave up on me to go for that guy.

His name was Steve and he worked as a security guard for the school she studied at. He was a tall black man, had short hair, used to have earrings and wear rings, had a tattoo of a Chinese dragon on his back, was well built, and, overall, looked like the kind of man I wouldn't want to piss off.

In fact, I never even protested when she announced our breakup. Jessica was with him and all I could do was run away crying back to my apartment. Steve was laughing and kissing her as he noticed his clear victory over me for her heart.

Ever since then, I had difficulty using porn websites to relieve my daily stress. Every now and then I would run into one of those videos of black men fucking white women and that always had the effect of immediately killing my mood. My mind would always think back to Jessica and how we used to love each other until big black Steve showed up.

Given that those videos bothered me a lot, I set in stone the objective to get over my hatred for black men in general that was caused by Steve. Not all of them were jerks as he was, and I had to remind myself of that.

In addition, it was ridiculous to stop enjoying porn because of a black guy who stole my girlfriend. Those men in the videos with their big black cocks standing proudly had nothing to do with what had transpired.

Initially, it looked like my plan would work. I clicked on some of those videos and forced myself to watch them. My mind would torment me by showing images of Jessica being impaled by Steve, though, which was mildly annoying.

Eventually, my mind learned not to sabotage me and, thus, I could enjoy watching black men dominating little white girls. Their cocks, which were usually a lot bigger than mine was, invigorated me.

As time passed, so did my hatred for Steve. I had finally accepted that I would never be on the same level. Steve was the kind of guy she deserved. Jessica was indeed too good for me. I learned I should be proud of myself for being with her during that short amount of time that we were together.

Curious as I was to watch newer videos of black men and after running out of the straight ones, I had to resort to the gay and bisexual categories. The first few videos left a disgusting taste in me, but at least my appetite for big black cocks humiliating smaller people was being satisfied.

Eventually, even that prejudice lost its strength in my mind. I became more willing to watch gay videos featuring black men as the protagonists. Their toned bodies and proud cocks ticked something in me I could not precisely describe.

Before I knew it, I was fully enjoying gay videos. Those smaller white men being fucked by much bigger black guys had the capacity to truly turn me on. I would always jerk off furiously before blowing a huge load over my carpet.

Said videos even became a favorite topic of mine on the internet. When I was done watching all the videos of a website, I would always look for other sources of content to satisfy my appetite.

I even went to the deep web to find more videos. I had to scroll down and ignore a bunch of pages of pedo stuff and the like to find what I was looking for, but the extra effort was always worth it in the end. There was something magical about being in the underworld of the internet trying to find something hidden behind layers of banned content and other stuff I would rather not remember.

A feeling of trying a big black cock eventually grew in me. It was small and almost unnoticeable during the first months, but it quickly grew into a monster I could not ignore.

I ended up buying a big black dildo to satisfy my desire, since I wasn't quite ready to deal with the real thing. My first attempts at trying to stick it up inside my asshole were nothing short of complete failures, since I was too afraid of the damage it would do to my virgin orifice.

Eventually, though, it got easier. The dildo fitted perfectly inside my dirty rectum. At the time, I still had not learned that cleaning that part of me was a thing.

The big black dildo kind of became a friend of mine. Every day after work I would play with it, suck its enormous cockhead for hours on end before sleeping with it stuck inside my asshole.

I was already well into gay sex; I just hadn't taken the next step to do it yet. It was then that I signed up on some gay dating websites. My favorite topics were, of course, searching for big black males who looked ready to ram my willing asshole.

I spent months just browsing those websites. The city I lived in had a sizable black male population, and since it was a metropolis, that meant I had an almost infinite pool of black guys to stalk every day.

I quickly became more willing to take things a step further. I configured my accounts to show that I was looking for a black man to dominate me all day long for the next Sunday. I even snapped some nudes or when I was wearing suggestive women's clothes like thongs to spice things up.

It didn't take long for my message folder to be bombarded by black men willing to do what I wanted. I savored and read carefully each of their messages before choosing the best of them.

His name was Steve, and I guess I chose him partially because his name was the same as that guy who took my girlfriend away from me. Steve was very similar physically to him as well: athletic body, chocolate skin, thick and red-hot lips, short hair, brown eyes, and tattoos all over his body.

CHAPTER 2

I was very amused once we started sharing messages.

"u gud 4 dis" was his first message.

"Yes, my butthole can't wait to meet your BBC. Just saw your latest pics. You look gorgeous."

"hehe, so wen can i meet u"

"How about this Sunday? I'm free and willing to do anything you want."

"sunday is gud and perfect for me. can't wait to get a taste & rim that asshole of yours. btw, where do you live"

"On Elmpalm Street, the house number is 489. It has a small front yard with some palm trees. It's a very simple house."

"gud gud dat is not far from where i live. i have seen some of your pics as well. can u send more. my cock's itching for new angles."

"Sure, what positions and angles do you want to see this time? Maybe a view from the floor of my much smaller cock standing proudly and leaking precum as I masturbate?"

"yes yes dat would be gud."

I grabbed my phone, opened the camera app, and set the timer to take three pictures while I stroked my cock to full hardness. Then, once it was done, I sent the pictures to Steve.

"looks gu, sweetheart. how about a couple more pictures of your asshole. try widening it a bit so that i can get a better picture of it."

"Sure, I can send those as well."

I grabbed my phone once again, put it on the floor, and lined my ass over it as I tried to widen my hole as much as I could. The camera app made three *beeping* sounds once the pictures were taken.

I sent him the pictures and he responded at the same instant.

"u looking gorgeous as ever. i'm jerking off violently as I savor these pics. you are one handsome twink. can't wait to send you to the moon with my oversized black cock."

"Oh, and as for me, I can't wait to finally get a taste of your big black cock. My former girlfriend kept telling me I would never want to go back after having such an experience."

"oh, u had a girlfriend? were u always bi?"

"No, I just recently discovered that I am. I had always thought of myself as being 100% straight, but recent events made me realize I'm much more than that."

"oh, I can't wait tah show yo what you've been missin this whole time. why did your girlfriend leave you?"

I didn't know if I should respond to him right away or just avoid the question, since my break up with my ex still hurt me. As I stood there with my ass on the chair, he sent another message.

"u still there?"

"Yes, I am. Sorry, it's just that I don't want to talk about my former girlfriend. It still hurts me the way she left."

"y", he probed. He wasn't about to let this topic go.

Taking a deep breath, I responded, "Because she left me for a big black man just like you. I didn't just feel betrayed, but I also felt extremely humiliated, you know? Deep down, I would have been more willing to accept our breakup if it wasn't with someone like him."

"u racist?"

I raced my fingers over the digital keyboard while trying to come up with an honest answer that would convince him. I knew I wasn't racist; I just worded my last message poorly. Steve left a scar in me I could never heal.

It was, actually, the fact that he was much taller, stronger, and had a cock inches longer and thicker than mine that made me feel tiny. I knew that, no matter how much I could improve, I would never reach the same level as the other Steve. Those factors were simply beyond my limits.

"No, I just felt… humiliated by a man I knew I could never defeat. He was much taller and stronger than I was. The levels of self-esteem I felt from him were intoxicating. His cock too… it must have been so much larger than mine that I felt meaningless in front of him. I felt frustrated for not having the capacity to get to his level. But yeah, I'm not racist."

"gud, dat actually makes me feel more excited for dis. i'm going to show you dat u can actually enjoy being dominated by a man much larger and better than u. prepare to worship my big black cock. I'm going now."

Then, I took another picture of my white ass and sent it to Steve to tell him I couldn't wait anymore for his arrival. Afterward, I turned off my phone and took a short nap.

My heart was beating fast in my chest. I was about to have my first gay sexual experience, and Steve had everything I needed.

CHAPTER 3

I was awakened by the sound of the doorbell being rung. My hand was still in my pants and caressing my cock. I quickly crawled out of the bed and headed downstairs to meet my guest.

My heart was still pounding faster than usual when I opened the door. I was able to see him from the glass of the door, but seeing him in person and in full glory was something else entirely.

Steve wasn't just tall; he was at least a head and half taller than I was. I literally had to lift my head to look him in the eye. I took a good look at him from top to bottom in order to get every little detail that enticed me.

Short hair, chocolate skin, athletic body, fairly hairy legs and arms, big hands and feet, thick lips, and, of course, a bulge that seemed to grow by the second. Every part of his body seemed to make me feel more excited and ready to let him dominate me.

Doing that last part was going to be easy for him, given the difference in stature between us. He probably weighed at least twice as much as I did and each of his arms was probably as thick as my torso. I was in heaven with this man.

"Please, come in", I said as I stood aside letting him get in.

"Nice den yo' have got here. R' yo' rich?"

"Yeah… I guess I kinda am."

That was the sort of thing I had never thought about before, but given my accumulated wealth, most would say I was indeed rich.

Having extra resources meant I could have things most people would never even dream of, and for that occasion, I suspected they would prove very beneficial.

"It's gettin' hot in here", Steve said while taking off his t-shirt. I could see more of his tattoos now. There was one of an angel on his arm and the name of someone on his back.

Curious about that last one, I asked, "Who's Stella?"

He turned around, clearly a bit surprised by my question, "Oh, her... just my fuckin' ex."

So he and I both had girlfriends before trying gay sex. How interesting that was. I wondered what happened between them, but I avoided probing the subject further because it was unimportant right now.

My mind was set on feasting on the big black cock he had between his legs. The bulge was big even under the grace of his basketball shorts. He drew a smile across his face once he noticed my eyes locked to his bulge.

Then, he grabbed at it sensually and asked, "Like what the fuck yo' peep at? How tha fuck 'bout we spice dis the fuck up a bit mo' instead o' havin' simple gay sex?"

"What do you mean?"

"I peep yo' have got an interestin' assortment o' items here. I could create some interestin' occasions dat gotta leave long-lastin' marks within our minds."

"Sure... I guess we can try that."

Even though I looked calm on the outside, the truth was that I was very nervous. I had never been that close to having gay sex and didn't know how things worked. I avoided bringing that topic up because I didn't want him knowing I was an amateur. That had the potential of ruining this perfect moment.

"But first, time ta warm the fuck up."

Warm up? I wondered what he meant, but then my question was quickly answered once he began to push down his shorts. They plummeted down to the floor and, then, he started to walk in my direction.

When he was just mere inches from me, his torso threatening

to engulf me with its enormous size, he said loudly, "Kneel, bi-atch."

The look on his face was very clear. He wasn't going to take no for an answer. Fear flared up in me and I could do nothing about it.

Once my face was in line with his boner, he said, "Suck it". It was a simple command and I thanked him for that. I was so nervous and my heart was beating so fast I couldn't think properly. My thoughts were being processed in a completely out-of-order fashion.

There was a distinct smell of musk surrounding his bulge, even though he had definitely taken a shower before showing up. The smell was intoxicating and lured me in. My head was moving on its own and, before I knew it, I was mouthing his cock through the fabric of his navy-blue boxer briefs.

"Not like that", he said before taking off his underwear and putting it on top of my head. The smell of musk was even more intoxicating without the briefs protecting his cock from my predatory mouth.

His cock was easily the biggest one I had ever seen in my life. The dildo I bought that day couldn't even be compared to it. The difference in size was staggering, and I stood there in awe just taking in on the size of his dick.

Then, Steve said with a slight hint of irritation in his voice, "Suck."

That was another simple command I was glad to obey. I grabbed his cock slowly with my hands and I noticed how smaller it was than his big black cock. I put each of my fingers on his man tool carefully since I felt that, at any moment, it could get a life of its own and take me by force.

Steve emitted a long groan when I wrapped my lips around the geometry of his cockhead. It was meaty and the leaking pre-cum was so juicy I wanted to drink all of it. I was mostly doing that instead of sucking the extremely smooth skin of his king cockhead.

During that moment, I realized that I was finally achieving an objective I had been seeking for a long time. I wanted to feel inferior and worship a man much bigger than I was, and there was no doubt that Steve was the perfect specimen for that.

Steve put one of his hands on my head and it enveloped the whole rounded-geometry with ease. The strength of his hand on my head was almost unnoticeable, but there was just enough of it to let him dictate the rhythm he wanted. Slowly, I sucked one-third of the length of his cock while he pushed and pulled my head.

"So good... yo' do dat shit so good", he said with his eyes closed and his head inclined backward.

Not only was his cock thick and long, but it was also veiny. Each of the veins was pulsing against the soft touch of my lips on the skin of his big black cock. The feeling was nothing short of enticing.

His cock and balls were getting increasingly hot under the tender touch of my lips as well. I could feel him getting closer to sharing his seeds with me, which was something I was dearly waiting for.

Before things could progress any further, though, he lifted his hand from my head and said, "Warm-up be done. Naw, time fo' tha real action."

His cock was quickly withdrawn from my mouth and I felt abandoned, maybe even betrayed by that sacrilegious act. Not only that, but his big man tool had also kind of calmed me down and made me feel safe. I instantly became nervous once again when I noticed I wasn't mouthing on his dick.

He noticed what I was feeling and said, "Come on, git the fuck up. There's mo' n' much better", before turning around and going to the kitchen.

Then, I heard my table being pushed and him getting the ladder I had outside in the garden. Just what did he have in mind?

I saw him getting back into the kitchen with the ladder on his shoulder when I crossed the corridor to get there. He quickly put the ladder in the center of the room and anchored two points with a long leather strap that was obviously going to be used as some sort of swing.

Then, he announced his plan, "Get undressed, biatch n' start swingin' wit' yo' asshole wide open fo' me."

I had no idea how I was going to do that. The whole thing was alien to me, and that unusual - yet creative - situation was completely different from everything I had seen in porn videos. Either way, I was excited.

I took off my clothes quickly and rested my white butt on the swing while trying to widen my asshole for him. Steve positioned himself behind me, his cock clearly aimed for my waiting orifice.

"I'm going to push you now!" he said while bursting out laughing. I felt my body being pushed with ease by his much stronger hands and then quickly going back toward his cock.

I was still trying to widen my asshole when I felt his cock instantly impaling me. The whole thing happened in a matter of seconds and I was taken by surprise when I felt his thick cock getting in without resistance from me. I screamed the moment I felt the tip of his cockhead breaking through my orifice like a hot knife cutting through butter.

Steve burst out laughing when he pushed me away on the swing a second time. I felt the breezing air cooling my body as the swing went in the opposite direction after reaching its limit and my asshole getting close to being impaled a second time by his big black cock.

This time I knew what to expect, but the pain was still as significant as before. His veiny, black cock broke through whatever insignificant resistance my orifice still had and widened my formerly virgin asshole even more.

"You like dat, don't yo'? So I gotta keep doin' dis until I'm satisfied!"

And he wasn't lying. He pushed me again and again. My rectum was being ravaged by his thick cock intermittently, and I was loving that. It was like being a kid again and being pushed by your father while playing with the swing, except that this time I was a grown-up and Steve wasn't my old man.

Steve was thrilled thanks to his creative way to rock me, and he didn't know he had just become the one who made me lose my ass virginity. He was laughing like a maniac while shoving me again and again.

Eventually, the pain decreased just enough to be unnoticeable and, thus, I stopped screaming. It took maybe ten minutes to get to that point, and thus Steve decided that he needed to up the heat.

Once I had been impaled by him for the last time on the swing, he held me in place with his hands against my arms and said, "Time fo' round two naw. I'm goin' ta git anotha long leatha strap so dat we can do somethang a bit different."

Again, I had no idea what he had in mind while he raced back outside and brought in another long leather strap. Then, he used the ladder another time to anchor the strap to the ceiling.

Afterward, he said, "Lay on top o' both straps belly down n' suck my cock while I push yo'. Dis goin' ta be like the fuck we just did. Tha difference be dat yo' gotta deep-throat now."

I had shivers just thinking about deep-throating a cock as long and thick as his was. I was confident I could do it, though, so I just laid belly-down on both straps and waited for him to start pushing me.

Again, he pushed me and I closed my eyes while keeping my mouth as open as I could for his cock. Once my body was going back the other way, I held myself tighter to the straps and enthusiastically waited for his dong to penetrate my mouth.

I felt his cock simply sliding in and going deep inside my throat when the swing swung back. Just feeling that enormous monstrosity getting in, its veins pulsing harder than ever, was enough to make me leak pre-cum all over the marble floor of the kitchen.

He did it again and again until I felt my throat sore. Each time his big black dong slid in with ease, I tried to suck as much as I could of it.

I had the desire to get a taste of his cock, but the swing always went in and out so fast that it was basically impossible to do so. This occasion was essentially a fancy way to tease me as much as he could.

Regardless, I was enjoying that because I had never imagined that two men could do such a thing. It was so genuinely new that I bet some people would even be inclined to come in and join us for the fun it was. Steve really seemed to have a knack for creating completely new positions for sex.

Then, once he had enough of that, he decided to change things up again. This time he took off the leather straps from the ceiling and asked, "Where's yo' bedroom?"

"Upstairs. Follow me."

With my fully naked body exposed to the cold air inside the house, I made my way to my bedroom. It was on the second floor and at the end of the hallway.

"Big place yo' have here", Steve commented while looking left and right in all the rooms we passed by. I was glad that he liked my place.

Once we got into the bedroom, Steve announced, "Lay on da bed on yo' back wit' yo' head hangin' a lil' off da edge by da sidewall. By doin' dat, I can balance against tha wall while I move down ova yo' face. I learned dis position wit' some o' da girls who did dat shitload o' times fo' me. I'm shizzle yo' gotta like dat shit."

I wasn't sure about what he wanted to do once I was in position, but I did what he asked anyway. My heart was still beating faster than usual while I waited for him to position himself behind me. I was having a bad case of cold sweat when I saw his big ass, cock, and scrotum a few inches from me.

After thinking that I was straight for so long, there I was doing whatever that big black man wanted. Using a makeshift swing while he rocked my butt and mouth? Check, I did that. Sucking his asshole, dick, and balls while I was on the bed with him behind me? Check, since there was no way I could simply say no and run away from him then. Doing what he wanted was going to make me lose even more of my dignity, and I loved that.

He lowered himself while using the wall to balance his body and now his large scrotum was within reach of my hands. I grabbed his ballsack and began to massage it tenderly. Steve moaned and groaned a lot while I did that, which was always a good incentive to keep going.

The smell of musk was even more saturated at that point. I almost forgot I was in my own bedroom while I admired and took in all that smell.

Meanwhile, his big black cock was still hard as a rock and leaking precum like a broken faucet. I just stood there taking in all of that juicy liquid while I massaged his big balls. The size of each of those was probably twice the size of my two testicles combined, which made me feel even more inferior to that beast of nature.

The muscles of his upper thighs and abs seemed to resonate with his exerted effort and my handiwork on his balls. Once I finally wrapped my pink-ish lips around each of them, the resonance became even more noticeable. It was as if those parts of him didn't fully belong to his body anymore.

The moment I put both of his balls inside my mouth, each of them occupying every possible space I had there, was when I knew I had reached one of the peaks of my humiliation and degradation. I was nothing but a little white man doing everything that a much bigger black guy wanted.

Steve was well-aware of such a condition when he lowered himself even further, thus putting his cock within reach of my hungry mouth.

I was so excited to finally have that big black cock inside my mouth when I wrapped my soft lips around the base of its purple cockhead. His member was still leaking pre-cum when I did that and, thus, I instantly felt the distinctive flavor of that liquid coming in contact with my taste buds.

I felt safe again once I had that cock inside my mouth. I was nothing but a little kid who liked his candy and wanted to keep it forever while knowing that doing so was impossible. In light of that, I held it closer and tighter between my lips as I tried to fight against that inevitable fact.

I was mouthing his cockhead feverously since that was the only thing I could do at the moment. I was swirling my tongue around the whole geometry and taking in the pulsing veins as much as I could.

That position was perfect for the moment of submission and degradation that Steve was aiming for.

Steve was, of course, an artist at that sort of thing. He always pushed away from my mouth when he wanted to tease me more. There was a constant struggle to keep as much of his meaty cock inside my mouth as he kept on trying to push it out. It was like fighting in a war I knew I couldn't win because my opponent had all the power.

When he was done with all the teasing, he lowered himself down even more, but then, when I was about to ease his whole cock inside my waiting mouth, he used his hand to grab his manhood and push it away from me.

I was slightly irritated when he did that, but that thought quickly faded when he offered me his perineum, which was the part between his asshole and his scrotum. That region was highly sensitive and could be enlarged depending on how aroused he was.

I raced my tongue over his perineum, making sure to hit all the sensitive sweet spots I knew he had there. Steve moaned louder and longer than ever, making me feel even more excited to keep going.

There was a very distinct taste that pertained to that region of his, and as far as my research told me, it was different for every man. It was similar to a person's digitals, except that it was a lot sexier.

Once he was satisfied with that, he squatted down further and now my face was buried deep between his buttcheeks. The smell of musk was even more intoxicating and it was basically the only thing I could feel at the moment.

My nose was so deep between his asscheeks that I had trouble breathing. I had to move my head slightly down to get some fresh air.

"Tough, huh? well shiiit, dat was just half o' tha fun", he said before going down farther.

There was only one way to get that massive man out of there, and I had confidence I could pull that off without significant complications.

With that in mind, I aimed my tongue to where his widened asshole was and started to massage it. Steve moaned loudly with each touch of my wet tongue. That was, as usual, a good incentive to keep going.

I even went as far as putting the tip of my tongue inside his hole. It was not dirty or anything of the sort. In fact, he had to have cleaned himself up well before coming to my house.

Each time my tongue touched the outside of his orifice, Steve moaned louder than usual. As a response to that, my cock grew harder and more pre-cum leaked out of it instantly.

We were both enjoying that, but it was time to move to the final act. Steve repositioned himself so that I could breathe normally again and then he offered his oversized black cock for my willing mouth. I didn't need a second invitation to grab it with my hands and guide it to my lips.

I wrapped them around the geometry of his purple cockhelmet and began to mouth it slowly while he balanced himself using the wall as support.

I slurped and savored as much as I could of his manhood before he reached his climax. There was just so much meat to taste that it was impossible to focus on just one region. I kept changing focus areas while trying, without success, to please all of his cock at the same time.

His scrotum begged for some attention from me as well, but since I didn't want to stop sucking the full length of his member, I had to multitask. I kept his manhood well taken care of inside my mouth while I caressed his big balls with my much smaller white hands. The difference in size when compared to my own man tools was simply staggering and a good reminder of how much better than me he was.

It didn't take him long to finally reach his climax after all the other things we did first. I felt his cock throbbing inside my mouth and violently shocking against the internal structure of my cheeks. Keeping it there was like keeping a wild animal inside a cage, but I did the best I could, and it proved to be efficient.

He sprayed and painted my mouth with his huge load. It didn't take him long to fill me up until I was forced to swallow all of his milk. I tasted as much as I could of his cum, and it was deliciously salty. My own cock was leaking more pre-cum than ever.

Once I thought he was done, I moved my lips away from his cock and pushed his member slightly to the side. But then, out of nowhere, he guided his cock to my face again and closed his eyes.

He was obviously far from being done with me when his big black dick began to shoot his cum all over my face. I had just about enough time to close my eyes before his shots started to disfigure me.

The shots were coming from all directions since not even Steve could control his manhood. The member was shaking and aiming randomly so much that some of his cum even stained the bedsheets and the floor of my bedroom.

That was far from anything I could have done myself. I barely had enough juice to cum once, much less to do so twice in a couple of seconds. As a black man, nature really helped to make him the beast he was, and I was kind of terrified of that.

Once he was done, he laid on my own bed without asking for permission and quickly fell asleep. I followed suit and rested my head on his hairy, strong chest. I fell asleep while caressing his rounded pecs and biceps.

CHAPTER 4

It wasn't hard to imagine what that sexual experience truly meant for me. I was well over all the obstacles that once held me back. I was free to do whatever I wanted and please whatever degenerate feelings I had.

As I closed the door for Steve, my eyes admiring his athletic body from top to bottom, I realized I was going to need more soon. The good news was that I kept his number, but the bad one was that only Steve could quench my carnal needs.

Humans were kind of funny in that regard: once we finally got what we wanted, we always strived for more. It was impossible to be fully satisfied with something forever, and that was true especially when it came to sexual desires.

As I walked back into my room, my thoughts now tracing back all the events that led to that new life of mine, I decided that soon I'd be doing it all over again.

The End

Find the next books in the series here:

2. Big Black AND NEEDY
3. Big Black AND THICK
4. Big Black AND ERECT

5. Big Black AND STRAIGHT
6. Big Black AND VEINY

And lastly, leave a review if you liked the book. It always helps me so much!

TEASER: BIG BLACK AND NEEDY

A BBC Interracial Story (African Treats - 2)

Ever since Steve left the house that day, I knew that I wanted more. Just sucking his cock and being his bitch was not enough for me. I wanted to reach new levels of humiliation and submission that only big black men could provide.

Days after my first gay sex experience, I tried calling Steve, but he was either out of reach or too busy with something else. I felt betrayed by those reactions because I thought he had truly liked me.

I had to give up on him after a few weeks of constant failures. I needed and wanted more big black cocks, and that was the only thing that could satiate my sexual desires. Jerking off furiously multiple times every day never had the same impact that Steve had.

Eventually, I gave up on him. I went to the internet to find other black men who were willing to make me their bitch just like Steve did. Unfortunately, even after all the invested efforts, nobody turned up. All the black men on those websites said they were "looking for something else."

I felt kind of expendable at that point. I was not their object of desire anymore; I was simply something they could use one day and put aside the day after. The worst was that there was nothing I could do about it. I was simply a little white man without a lot of value for them.

The days without a big black man were very hard. I felt abandoned and alone. Steve and his black power made me feel safe. I had found true happiness when he allowed me to suck his scrotum while squatting over my head. That sort of feeling was impossible to achieve without another black man like him.

The days without hope were numbered, though. I eventually found the benefits of the deep web. There were, of course, the despicable pages featuring things that made me puke, but there were more and bigger websites for people like me.

The best thing about said pages was their diversity. There were so many of them telling about places in the city where a white man could suck a black guy's cock after paying for it. I had the money and the free time, so doing that was a no brainer for me.

The only thing I hadn't made my mind on, however, was where I would go to suck a black man's cock. There was a cinema in one of the poorest neighborhoods in the city, a football stadium and a shady barbershop. I had time for just one of them for the next Sunday.

Since the cinema was relatively well known and there were many positive reviews for it than for the other places, I decided to go there. It was not far from my house as well; the trip would take roughly twenty minutes by car.

The place was known for allowing white men like me to suck big black guys while they watched some naughty movies. From the outside, the structure looked nothing like that of a cinema, but it was clear the place was famous.

Before going there, however, I decided to sign-up on their website to chat with one of the staff members – or maybe even one of the clients – to get a better picture of the place. I liked doing that sort of "investigation" because it helped to set me in the mood…

MORE BBC AND GAY STORIES

SERIES - AFRICAN DELIGHT

1. BBC Creams On Me: A Straight to Gay MM Story
2. BBC Takes Me: A Straight to Gay MM Story
3. BBC Claims Me: A Straight to Gay MM Story

STRAIGHT TO GAY BUNDLES

1. Not Entirely Straight: Straight to Gay First Time
2. Throbbing Hard: A Straight to Gay MMF Bundle
3. Hard to Please: A Straight to Gay MM Bundle
4. Barging In: 7 Straight to Gay MM Stories
5. Making it Stretch: A Straight to Gay MM Bundle

ABOUT THE AUTHOR

Steamy MM stories, baby! Michael Levi can't go a day without sitting down and putting into words all the dirty scenes that sprout in his mind. His collection is diverse, but it's gay love only. You won't find anything else on his author page. And if you're looking for something free, check his mailing list. Warning: it can be extra spicy.

When he isn't writing, he's chilling out by the lake close to his house. Nothing better than kicking back with a martini in his hand as he dreams if he'll ever find the man he wants.

www.ingramcontent.com/pod-product-compliance
Lightning Source LLC
Chambersburg PA
CBHW052138150726
48002CB00006B/2668